Powder and Patch

Georgette Heyer

arrow books

Published by Arrow Books in 2005

7 9 10 8 6

First published in the United Kingdom as *The Transformation of Philip Jettan* in 1923 by
Mills and Boon.

New edition published in 1930 by William Heinemann

Arrow Books
Random House, 20 Vauxhall Bridge Road,
London SW1V 2SA

www.rbooks.co.uk

Addresses for companies within The Random House Group Limited
can be found at: www.randomhouse.co.uk/offices.htm

The Random House Group Limited Reg. No. 954009

A CIP catalogue record for this book
is available from the British Library

ISBN 9780099474432

The Random House Group Limited supports The Forest
Stewardship Council (FSC), the leading international forest
certification organisation. All our titles that are printed on
Greenpeace approved FSC certified paper carry the FSC logo.
Our paper procurement policy can be found at
www.rbooks.co.uk/environment.

Typeset by SX Composing DTP, Rayleigh, Essex
Printed in Great Britain by CPI Bookmarque, Croydon, CR0 4TD